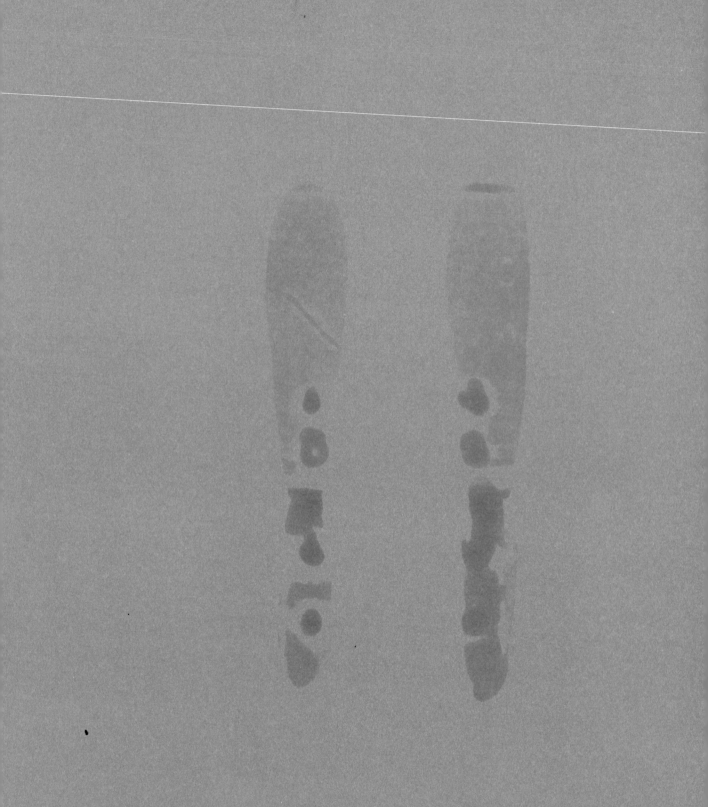

What Rhymes with
MOON?

What Rhymes with MOON?

Jane Yolen

ILLUSTRATIONS BY
Ruth Tietjen Councell

Philomel Books · New York

For Steve and Maria,
and all the moons
over Rio

J.Y.

For Martha Anne

R.T.C.

Text copyright © 1993 by Jane Yolen.
Illustrations copyright © 1993 by Ruth Tietjen Councell.
All rights reserved. This book, or parts thereof, may not be reproduced
in any form without permission in writing from the publisher.
Philomel Books, a division of The Putnam & Grosset Group,
200 Madison Avenue, New York, NY 10016. Published simultaneously in Canada.
Printed in Hong Kong by South China Printing Co. (1988) Ltd.
The text is set in Kennerley. Lettering by David Gatti.
The artist used watercolors mixed with opaque white to create
the illustrations for this book.

Library of Congress Cataloging-in-Publication Data Yolen, Jane.   What rhymes with moon? / by
Jane Yolen; illustrated by Ruth Tietjen Councell.   p.   cm.   Summary: Presents nineteen poems,
such as "Brazilian Moon Tale," "Green Cheese," and "Grandmother Moon," which in some way
relate to the moon.   1. Moon—Juvenile poetry.   2. Children's poetry, American. [1. Moon—
Poetry.   2. American poetry.]   I. Councell, Ruth Tietjen, ill.   II. Title.   PS3575.O43W46
1993   811'.54—dc20   92-7439   CIP   AC   ISBN 0-399-22501-3

"Father Wolf's Midnight Song" first appeared in *Dragon Night and Other Lullabies,*
© 1980 by Jane Yolen, published by Methuen, Inc.
"The Cow Who Jumped" first appeared in *Isaac Asimov's Science Fiction Magazine.*
"Dream Maker" first appeared in *Cricket.*

1   3   5   7   9   10   8   6   4   2

First Impression

Contents

When I was a child growing up in New York City, I slept in a back bedroom. My windows overlooked an alley and I could never see the moon. I had nightmares all the time and believed that there were wolves under my bed and a great black bear in my closet. Getting up in the middle of the night to go to the bathroom was an agonizing adventure.

When we moved to the country, my bedroom windows looked out over trees and grass and flowers and, in the wintertime, the snow-covered lawn. I could see the moon. And seeing the moon, I stopped being afraid of the night. In fact, I would often sit at my window and look up at the moon imagining that—well, imagining all sorts of things.

These poems, written over a period of ten years, come out of all those moon imaginings. And if they make the nighttime a happier, safer, more magical time for you, then I am satisfied.

—*Jane Yolen*

What Rhymes with Moon?

What rhymes with moon?
Not cheese, not sky,
Not a sprinkle of stars,
Not a blind white eye,
Not a worn, thin coin,
Not a cracker, not a pie,
Not an old man's face,
Not you, not I.

What rhymes with moon?
Not a thing that means
What moonshine is
Or moonlight seems.
Only June and spoon
And tune
          and such.
What rhymes with moon?

Not much.

The Moon Is a Sickle

The moon is a sickle
For pruning the stars,
For thinning out Venus
And weeding out Mars,

For tidying Neptune
And reaping the sky.
The moon is a sickle,
And now you know why.

Moon in the Pond

Moon.

There are two, now,
One above,
hanging,
a globe, a lamp,
lighting the way.
The other a paten,
a plate, a tea tray,
almost within reach.

Moon.

Some Say

Some say the moon is silver.
Some say a cheesy green.
Some say the moon reflects the sun
And that is how it's seen.

But I know it's a mirror
And every time I stare
Into the moon's bright surface
I see my own self there.

The Cow Who Jumped

She jumped and below her
the careful pleats of the farm,
the ribbons of fences,
the mountains hemming the sea
fell away.

She jumped and the blue globe
was a button beneath her.

She jumped and the stars
like so many rhinestones
were flung against
the velvet cloth
of sky.

Her leap was a pattern
for the rest of us.

We *sew* ourselves into space.

Cutting Hair

In Devonshire, the farmers say
The waning moon marks trimming day.

In Worcestershire, a different tune—
They cut hair at the waxing moon.

If farmers all cannot agree
Which moon time cutting hair should be,

Then how can folk in different climes
Agree on any kind of times?

Cut too late or cut too soon
When calculated by the moon.

Before you know it, we could be
Smack in a hair catastrophe.

Some cutters might get much too careless.
Perhaps we'd better all go hairless.

Old Woman Who Never Dies

The Sioux knew the way of it.
Old Woman Who Never Dies
They called the moon,
Staring up into the night sky
While all around, the dark whispered
In many little voices.

It is hard to hear
Those voices now,
With the streetlights shouting,
With the traffic lights shouting,
With the house lights,
Car lights,
TV lights shouting.

Go away from the city.
Go away from the town.
Go out into the prairie.
Go out into the desert.
Go out upon the water.
Look up at the Old Woman.
She never dies.

She will whisper to you
With the little voices of the night.
Swee-swash sings the grass.
Cree-up sing the frogs.
Lip-lap sings the water.
Pick-buzz sing the tiny wings
Of the thousand thousand
Brothers of the air.

Tree Lullabies: Haiku

Oak

Acorn sleep over,
The oak pulls up its root-straps,
Dancing to the moon.

Willow

On the moon river,
Green hair and green reflections,
She dreams of—herself.

Birch

Side by side they rest,
Groomless brides in the moonlight,
White ladies sleeping.

Aspen

The moon sends no wind.
The quaking aspen trembles,
Sleep is in the seed.

21

Somebody Told Me Once

Somebody told me once
people used to believe
the moon was where we sent
everything that got broke on earth:
my Barbie doll without its arm;
the football that popped
when Strider grabbed it with his teeth;
Mama's cloth unicorn
that lost its horn;
Dad's eyeglasses he wore
with the Band-Aid
holding both sides together;
and all the little otters
mucked up with oil
I saw on TV.
Maybe we get all the moon's
unwanted stuff in exchange.
That would explain
creamed spinach,
anchovies dropped on pizza,
Mrs. Ashkenazi
who taught me second grade,
and any book to be found
in the dentist's waiting room.

Dream Maker

The shining silver moon
Is a coin hung in the sky
To pay the old Dream Maker
Whenever he goes by.

Mr. Mooney

Mr. Mooney sits all alone
on a park bench,
his fat old face sorry
and his eyes half closed.
Around him children
cry "Ring-a-leery-o"
and "Catch me if you can"
and he remembers when.

Green Cheese

You moldy old moon,
You lump of green cheese,
You heap of dirty clothes
With baggy draggy knees.

We left you out so long,
I wonder—do you smell?
I've not yet been
Quite close enough to tell.

Father Wolf's Midnight Song

The east wind is up
And the jackrabbit flees.
Cast for the scent
That still clings to the trees.

Howl, wolves, and sing to the moon.

The air is our map
And the scent points the way.
Up, pack, and out, pack,
And follow the prey.

Sing, wolves, for morning comes soon.

The hunt is our dream time
And day is our night.
We slip through the starshine,
We sleep through the light.

Howl, wolves, and sing to the moon.
Sing, wolves, for morning comes soon.

Brazilian Moon Tale

Did you hear the one
about the moon
being nibbled, gnawed,
eaten away,
by a rat, a jaguar,
a lion, until
in one great gulp
it was gone?

I didn't believe it
either,
until I looked up
and saw that moon,
the teethmarks
still on it,
growing smaller every night.

Moon Writing

What is written
across the moon's face?
A trace of owl,
like a single word;
a race of geese,
two lines of a verse.
Then a spaceship,
the exclamation point,
that marks the end
of moon writing,
and the beginning of man's.

The Astronaut Sings
Back to the Moon

I sing of your craters,
I sing of your dry seas
calling to me as the ocean
long ago sang to sailors.
I have no mast for binding
when your siren songs
try to pull me from my craft;
only the earphones
where the voices of Central
speak to me of earth things:
measurements, years,
the unfolding power of buds,
my children's tears,
whether the Celtics will win,
the ending to a joke,
my wife's misplaced car keys,
the real name of Briar Rose.
All those simple things
call me home, bind me to the past
as surely as Odysseus was bound to his mast.

Mama, Mama, Catch Me a Star

Mama, Mama, catch me a star,
A star that is silvery bright,
To hang on a chain,
A long, linking chain
To go 'round my neck through the night.

Mama, Mama, catch me a moon,
A moon that is yellow and gleams,
To sit by my side,
A-lit by my side
To chase away all my bad dreams.

Mama, Mama, catch me a cloud,
A cloud that is feathery white,
To lie on my bed,
Right under my head,
To pillow my head through the night.

Mama, Mama, catch me some rain,
And rainbows of shimmering light,
To drip in my glass,
To sip from my glass
In case I get thirsty at night.

Mama, Mama, catch me a wind
Out of the whispering skies
So I can hear
Right in my ear
All of the night's lullabies.

35

Christmas Eve: Hatfield

So we come at last to the country
Silent under its whited sheets
Where ice hangs down the wires
Like crystallized Christmas treats;

The moon so round and solid,
A gold ornament in the sky.
And the soft *shu-shush* of our tires
As we pass the Center by.

It is all as perfect as a picture
Illustrating a favorite poem
Where an angel, straight as a weather vane,
Points north-northeast toward home.

Grandmother Moon

Each day is a journey,
a leaving home,
over paths that wind
between rocks and bog.
Behind each rock
is a shadow;
behind each shadow,
a flower,
or a wellspring,
or a trembling rabbit,
or an unfolding fern.
Only if you look
will you find.
Only if you leave
will you arrive.
One step,
then another,
as day unrolls itself
along the road toward night.

And at evening,
look who welcomes us—
Grandmother Moon,
waiting in the doorway,
the stars in her hands—
to lead us safely home.